SLOTH GETS BUSY

A book about feeling Lazy

Written by Sue Graves

Illustrated by Trevor Dunton

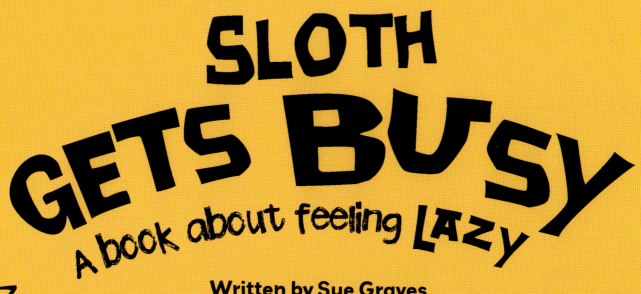

W
FRANKLIN WATTS
LONDON • SYDNEY

Sloth was very lazy. His bedroom was a mess.
He **never hung up** his clothes.
He **never tidied away** his toys.
Mum said he should help more.
But Sloth said tidying up was **boring**.

Once when it was Tiger's birthday party,
Sloth wanted to wear his favourite tee-shirt.
But he couldn't find it in all the mess.

So he had to go to the party in his worst jumper instead. Mum said if he **put things away properly**, he'd be able to find everything.

Every morning, Sloth's mum and dad tried hard to get Sloth out of bed. Mum tried making a lot of noise. But that was no good.

Dad tried to **pull him out**. But that didn't work either. Dad said he was **lazy**.

Sloth said he liked his comfy bed too much.

He didn't want to get out of it ever!

Sloth **never helped** at home.
He **never washed up** his bowl and mug.
He couldn't be **bothered** to put his rubbish
in the bin. Mum and Dad got cross. They said
he was too lazy.

Sloth was lazy at school, too.
He couldn't **be bothered** to write neatly.
Miss Bird said she couldn't read his writing.
She said he'd have to write it again.

He couldn't **be bothered** to put the top on his water bottle. When he accidentally knocked it over, water went everywhere. Miss Bird said he had to mop up all the mess.

At playtime, everyone played football.
Sloth was in goal. But he soon **got bored**.
He had nap in the sunshine instead.
Everyone was cross that Sloth didn't want
to **join in**. They were cross he had
spoiled their game.

14

That afternoon, Miss Camel asked everyone
to make cupcakes for the school fair tomorrow.
She said the cake stall was always very popular.

She showed them how to make the cakes.
She told everyone to **clean up any spills**
straight away. She said spilling things on the floor
could be **dangerous**.

But Sloth didn't take any notice. He dropped
an egg. It spun across the floor and broke
right by Miss Camel's feet. Sloth couldn't be
bothered to clear up the mess.

Miss Camel didn't see the egg and she slipped
on it. She hurt her knee. Sloth felt bad.
He wished he'd cleared up the mess.
He was upset that Miss Camel was hurt.

Sloth went to see Miss Bird. He told her he was sorry for being so lazy. He wished he hadn't hurt Miss Camel. He wished he hadn't spoiled his friends' game. He wished he helped his mum and dad more, too.

Miss Bird asked him what he could do
to **put things right**. Sloth had a think.
He said he could **join in more** and **say
sorry**. He said he could **help other people**.
Miss Bird said they were
very good ideas.

Sloth said **sorry to everyone**. He **joined in** the football game and didn't stop for a nap once. Everyone said he was the best goalkeeper ever.

He wrote a card to Miss Camel to say sorry.
He did his **best writing**. Miss Camel said
it was the neatest writing she had seen.

At home time, Sloth said he was sorry
to Mum and Dad for being so lazy.
He **helped wash up**.

He **tidied** his room.
He **put away** all
his clothes.

He even **helped** wash the car.

Then Dad helped Sloth make lots of cupcakes for the school fair. Sloth made them carefully. He **cleared up** any spills.

The next day was the school fair.
Sloth **worked hard** all day.
Everyone said he was **very helpful**.
Sloth was pleased. He liked being busy.
He liked joining in. He said being lazy
was boring. It was much **nicer** to be busy
and to help others.

A note about sharing this book

The *Behaviour Matters* series has been developed to provide a starting point for further discussion on children's behaviour both in relation to themselves and others. The series is set in the jungle with animal characters reflecting typical behaviour traits often seen in young children.

Sloth Gets Busy
This story looks at the importance of not being lazy but of joining in and helping others.

The book aims to encourage the children to examine their own behaviour towards others and also to consider how this can affect their own happiness.

How to use the book
The book is designed for adults to share with either an individual child, or a group of children, and as a starting point for discussion.

The book also provides visual support and repeated words and phrases to build reading confidence.

Before reading the story
Choose a time to read when you and the children are relaxed and have time to share the story.

Spend time looking at the illustrations and talk about what the book might be about before reading it together.

Encourage children to employ a phonics first approach to tackling new words by sounding the words out.

After reading, talk about the book with the children:

- Talk about the story with the children. Ask them to describe Sloth's behaviour at the start of the book. Ask them how he behaves by the end of the book. Which type of behaviour do the children think is better and why?

- Ask the children why they think it is important to join in with others. Does it help make friendships? Does it make a game more fun if more people are involved?

- Ask the children what they do to help at home. Do they put their toys away? Do they keep their bedrooms tidy and do they hang up their clothes? Do they help Mum or Dad? Why do they think it is important to help at home?

- Place the children into groups. Ask them to list all the things they could do to help others both at home and at school.

- At the end of the session, invite a spokesperson from each group to read out their list to the others. Invite the children to help you design a poster showing how everyone can help at home and at school and place on display for future reference.

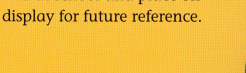

29

For Isabelle, William A, William G, George, Max, Emily,

Leo, Caspar, Felix, Tabitha, Phoebe and Harry – S.G.

Franklin Watts
First published in Great Britain in 2020
by The Watts Publishing Group

Text © Franklin Watts 2020
Illustrations © Trevor Dunton 2020

The right of Trevor Dunton to be identified as the illustrator
of this Work has been asserted in accordance with the
Copyright, Designs and Patents Act, 1988.

Editor: Jackie Hamley
Designer: Cathryn Gilbert

A CIP catalogue record for this book is available
from the British Library.

ISBN 978 1 4451 6865 4 (hardback)
ISBN 978 1 4451 6866 1 (paperback)

Printed in China

Franklin Watts is a division of
Hachette Children's Books,
an Hachette UK company.
www.hachette.co.uk

FSC
www.fsc.org

MIX
Paper from
responsible sources
FSC® C104740